A Concert in the Sand

This
PJ BOOK
belongs to

_____

_____

PJ Library®
JEWISH BEDTIME STORIES and SONGS

KAR-BEN PUBLISHING, INC.
A division of Lerner Publishing Group, Inc.
241 First Avenue North
Minneapolis, MN 55401 USA
1-800-4-KARBEN
Website address: www.karben.com

Main body text set in Rockwell Std Regular 15/19.
Typeface provided by Monotype Typography.

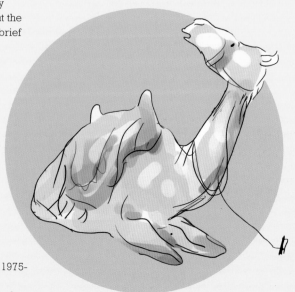

Library of Congress Cataloging-in-Publication Data

Names: Shem-Tov, Tami, 1969- author. | Sandbank, Rachella, author. | Ofer, Avi, 1975-
    illustrator.
Title: A concert in the sand / by Tami Shem-Tov and Rachella Sandbank ; illustrated
    by Avi Ofer.
Other titles: Kontsert ba-holot. English
Description: Minneapolis : Kar-Ben Publishing, [2017] | Translation of: Kontsert
    ba-holot / me-et Tami Shem -Tov ve-Rahelah Zandbank. —Yerushalayim, 2013. |
    Summary: "In 1936 Tel Aviv, a boy accompanies his grandmother on a walk along
    the beach, buying seltzer, looking in shops, talking with friends, and following men
    with strange-shaped cases. They end by meeting violinist Bronislaw Huberman
    and seeing the first performance of the Israel Philharmonic Orchestra"—Provided
    by publisher.
Identifiers; LCCN 2016009540 (print) | LCCN 2016034160 (ebook) | ISBN
    9781512400991 (lb : alk. paper) | ISBN 9781512401011 (pb : alk. paper) | ISBN
    9781512427189 (eb pdf)
Subjects: LCSH: Huberman, Bronislaw—Juvenile fiction. | Tizmoret ha-filharmonit
    ha- Yi´ssre'elit—History—Juvenile fiction. | CYAC: Huberman, Bronislaw—
    Fiction. | Israel Philharmonic Orchestra—History—Fiction. | Musicians—Fiction.
    | Grandmothers—Fiction. | Beaches—Fiction. | Jews—Palestine—Fiction. |
    Palestine—History—1917-1948—Fiction.
Classification: LCC PZ7.1.S514 Co 2017 (print) | LCC PZ7.1.S514 (ebook) | DDC
    [E]—dc23

LC record available at https://lccn.loc.gov/2016009540

Manufactured in China
1-38936-20910-9/29/2016

041720.6K1/B1039/A6

A Concert in the Sand

Tami Shem-Tov and Rachella Sandbank
English text based on translation by Nancy Wellins

Illustrations by **Avi Ofer**

KAR-BEN
PUBLISHING

It's boring hanging out at Mom and Dad's delicatessen.
Lots of construction workers come in to buy sandwiches
for lunch, so my parents don't have time for me.
My grandma has time. But she only speaks German.
And I don't.

Grandma shrugs and smiles as she waits for me by the door.
"Grandma and I are going out," I say.
"Where to, Uri?" Mom asks.
"Where to, Grandma?" I ask turning toward her.
But she's already out the door, so off I go too.

Where does Grandma want to go?
Ah, of course, the beach.
I take her hand as we head toward the sparkling sand.
There it is! The great blue sea of Tel Aviv. Fishermen
are casting their lines into the water.
Too bad we can't go swimming—it's wintertime now.

Grandma gazes out into the distance. What is she thinking about? The house where she grew up? The friends she knew long ago?

Back on the street, I see two men in coats
pass by carrying funny-shaped cases.
Grandma points at them and starts walking.

Where does Grandma want to go?

Ah, of course! She wants some seltzer.

We stop at a kiosk. A man is buying a raspberry seltzer. Grandma gets an apricot seltzer—my favorite! She hands me the cup.

The man joins the other two men, and Grandma continues walking.

Where are we going now?

Grandma is walking quickly. Maybe she's following the men with the funny-shaped cases. Maybe she likes pretending to be a spy, like I do. There's nobody like Grandma!

As we walk down the street, something strange happens. More men carrying funny-shaped cases appear. They shake hands and laugh with the others. I stop so they won't realize we're following them. Grandma stops too, and we peer into the display window of Mr. and Mrs. Gross' bookstore.

"That's my favorite book," I say, pointing to *Robinson Crusoe*. Grandma already knows that.

"Come on, Uri," she says.

The men with the funny-shaped cases are moving on too.

As we make our way through the park, I spot Danny and Aaron from my class hanging upside down on the monkey bars. I join them. Suspended between heaven and earth, I see the world upside down. Even Grandma is upside-down; she's sitting on a bench, chatting with a friend. They both have the exact same hairdo.

Three more people carrying funny-shaped cases now cross the park.

A leap, a jump, and Grandma and I are right behind them.

Why is Grandma stopping now?

Oh, to check out the new apartment building that's being built. When I saw it last week, it had only two stories—but now it has three! I look up and see workers shimmy down ropes to reach the ground. What fun that must be! I'd like to join them.

They brush the dust off their clothes. One puts on a hat, the other a jacket; then they set off on foot.

Where are they headed?

The street is getting crowded. Everyone is heading in the same direction. Fishermen and construction workers and the guy who sells seltzer at the kiosk, Mr. and Mrs. Gross from the bookstore with their dog, boys and girls, and Grandma and me. Leading the crowd is the group of people carrying the funny-shaped cases.

We have become a parade!

A man in a brown coat is attracting a lot of attention. Everyone wants to talk to him. Is he important?

Grandma walks toward him. Does she know him?

Suddenly, the man spots her. As he comes to greet her, other people stop him, patting him on the shoulder and chatting with him in different languages. "Mazel tov. Good luck, Mr. Huberman!" they say.

Mr. Huberman comes over to Grandma and they shake hands. They speak in German, and then Mr. Huberman looks at me and pats me on the head.

"Ah, so you're the grandson," he says. "I know your grandmother from a time long ago, when we were both living in Europe."

"This is Uri," Grandma introduces me proudly.

"I'm happy that you've both come," Mr. Huberman says. But before I can ask, "Come for *what?*" Mr. Huberman has vanished into the crowd.

The parade reaches a big auditorium
and everyone crowds inside.
The people with the cases go up onto
the stage and take their seats.

We find a place on one of the benches facing the stage. A man wearing glasses takes a violin out of his case. A tall woman puts together her clarinet. A bald man takes out his drum, while another with curly hair tunes his cello. A small woman with big cheeks lifts her trumpet.

The auditorium grows quiet. The mayor comes out on the stage. He welcomes the audience, praises the orchestra, and says to Mr. Huberman, "Thank you for bringing these excellent musicians together to create this orchestra for us."

The audience rises with a standing ovation. The applause goes on and on and on.

Mr. Huberman gazes out at the crowd with great emotion. Everyone is still clapping, together with the musicians, as Mr. Huberman takes his place on the stage and slips his violin between his shoulder and chin.

Famous Mr. Huberman knows my grandma, I think proudly to myself.

The concert is about to begin. A man with a little stick approaches the podium. He is the conductor, Arturo Toscanini. He pauses for a moment, and then gives the orchestra a signal.

The music of the orchestra quickly fills the auditorium. The notes enter my ears, and go straight to my heart. I turn and see that the same thing is happening to everyone. I didn't know that music could create such a feeling.

Grandma puts her hand on mine. She has tears in her eyes. I know that they are tears of happiness.

Historical Note

A Concert in the Sand tells the story of the first performance of what was to become the Israel Philharmonic Orchestra in Tel Aviv in December, 1936.

The orchestra was founded by Bronislaw Huberman (1882-1947), a Polish Jew who was identified at a young age as a musical prodigy and who later became a world-renowned violinist.

With the rise of the Nazis and the expulsion of Jewish musicians from German orchestras, Huberman understood that the future of the Jews of Europe was in peril. He traveled across Europe conducting orchestral auditions and chose some 70 outstanding Jewish musicians and traveled with them to Israel where they became the first members of the Israel Philharmonic Orchestra.

◀ *Bronislaw Huberman, playing violin*

▼ *Arturo Toscanini and Bronislaw Huberman after the first Palestine Symphony concert in December, 1936. This orchestra was to become the Israel Philharmonic.*

About the Author

Tami Shem-Tov was born in Kiryat Ono, Israel, and lives in Tel Aviv. She teaches creative writing at the University of Haifa. Her award-winning children's books include *Letters from Nowhere* and *I'm not a Thief*.

Rachella Sandbank was born in Jerusalem. She is the Children's and Young Adult books editor at Keter Books, one of the leading publishing houses in Israel. She lives in Hod HaSharon.

About the Illustrator

Illustrator and animation director **Avi Ofer** creates projects for a variety of media, including book and editorial illustration as well as direction of animated films. He has exhibited in art shows and screened in festivals around the world. He lives in Barcelona, Spain.